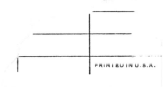

PRINTED IN U.S.A.

HI TOM

HI TOM

by NANDA WARD

Pictures by Lynd Ward

Hastings House Publishers

NEW YORK 22

1.85

Subscription

6/62

THOMAS THOMPSON was called "Thomas" by his pa, "Tommy" by his ma, and just plain "Tom" by his friends. The only time he saw his friends, though, was at school. They all lived down in Lonesome Valley while Tom and his ma and pa lived by themselves clear across Lonesome Valley and nearly to the top of Hermit Mountain.

7

Hermit Mountain was kind of a fearsome place. Whenever the wind blew gently in the valley, it was a gale up on the mountain. When the snow fell quietly in the valley, it was a blizzard up on the mountain side. And when there was a rainstorm in Lonesome Valley nowhere in the whole county was there such rumbling, bumping, crashing thunder and lightning as rolled around Hermit Mountain!

Some of the valley people said that when bad weather blew down their way it was because the Old Man of the Mountain was stompin' up a storm. It made Tom wonder. Of course, neither he nor his ma nor pa had ever seen an Old Man of the Mountain but that didn't mean there couldn't be one.

One thing was certain and agreed upon by all. Nowhere in the whole county were there such beautiful vegetables as Tom's pa grew up on the mountain and sold in the valley—nor any half as large. And the same held true for the skins of the animals Tom and his pa trapped each winter and brought down to the valley each spring.

10

So Tom liked living up on Hermit Mountain except for one thing. He sure wished he had someone to talk to on his long walk home from school each day. Tom had a hound dog named Trailer who walked to school with him, slept in the sun in the schoolyard, and walked back home with him when school was out. Old Trailer was the best hunting and tracking dog in the county and Tom was glad for his company. Still and all, there were times when Tom felt more lonesome than the valley itself as he said good-bye to his friends and started for home.

One such day Tom decided to take a new and different trail up Hermit Mountain. The trail wound around and around as Tom climbed higher and higher, then came out onto a wide, open space on the far side of Hermit Mountain. All around him Tom could see the tops of other mountains with deep ravines and crevices in between.

"Gosh all hemlock," Tom said to Trailer. "There's Blueberry Mountain, Blackberry Mountain, Raspberry Mountain, Strawberry Mountain and Elderberry Mountain! I've heard tell of them but I've never seen them before."

Trailer wagged his tail happily and gave a short bark. "Rrrrarf!" he yelped.

No sooner had he done so than his bark came back at him: "rrarf, RRarf, rrrrrarf, arf, RRRRARF!"

Trailer jumped behind Tom with his ears up and his tail down.

Tom laughed and scratched his dog's head. "Don't be scared, old boy, that's just an echo," he explained.

Trailer lifted his tail a little.

"Listen," said Tom. "I'll make some more echoes."

He took a deep breath, rar'ed back, and shouted: "Hi Tom!"

Instantly there came back from every mountain nook and cranny: "hi Tom, Hii Tomm, HI TOM, hiii tom, HIIIII TOMMM!"

Trailer perked up his ears again in surprise, then sat down and grinned as Tom went on calling out "Hi Tom" and listening to the echoes.

14

Having so many echoes bouncing around him made Tom feel as if some of his friends were standing on the mountaintops shouting a welcome to him. A smile spread across Tom's face and grew wider and wider as the echoes grew louder and louder. They made him forget the long walk across Lonesome Valley and up Hermit Mountain with no one to talk to.

As the sun dipped over the rim on Elderberry Mountain to the west, Tom picked up his books and ran on home to help his pa with the chores. Trailer loped along after him sniffing hopefully for the scent of a rabbit on the damp woods trail. As they came out of the woods they could see a warm yellow light shining from the windows of the cabin and Tom knew from the fragrance in the air his mother was fixing spoon bread, ham hocks, and turnip greens for supper.

16

When Tom went to bed that night there was
still a wide smile on his face as he remembered
the echoes on the far side of the mountain. Even
Trailer grinned in his sleep as he lay on the
rug beside Tom's bed.

Every day from then on, Tom went home from
school by way of his "echo place" as he called
it. Every day he bounded up the trail to the far
side of Hermit Mountain, took a deep breath,
rar'ed back and cried out "HIII TOMM" to
all the surrounding mountaintops. Every day
his voice grew stronger and stronger while the
echoes grew louder and louder.

17

Now, there was an old man living in a large cave on the far side of Hermit Mountain. He was the hermit the mountain had been named for. He was also the Old Man of the Mountain the people in the valley talked about. Because he had lived on the mountain so long, that hermit knew how to make the wind blow, the rain fall or the snow fly whenever he wanted them to!

Every day he took a nap that lasted all the way from lunch until suppertime. He loved to sleep and he hated to be awakened by anyone or anything. The old hermit had a very bad temper and all the birds and animals had learned to stay away from that cave while he slept.

18

In the beginning Tom's echoes didn't bother the old man much. He was a sound sleeper and his cave was a little distance from Tom's echo place. But one day Tom rar'ed back and gave such a bellow that the echoing "HIIIII TOMMM" rocked the whole mountain side and shook the hermit out of his bed of pine boughs.

"Dag nab it," fumed the old man. "Can't I ever get any peace and quiet?"

Presently everything was still so he clambered back onto his bed to try to get some sleep again.

20

No sooner had he closed his eyes, however, than once more "HIIIIII TOMMM" echoed across ravines and through gullies, bouncing him out of bed. This time the old hermit was beside himself with rage as he clomped around his cave to see where the noise came from. The more he looked the less he found, and the old hermit grew madder and madder.

"I'll give it just one more try," he growled warningly after a few moments of utter silence, "but if I'm woken up once again—"

He didn't finish his sentence as he climbed back onto the pine boughs but there was a fiery glint in his eye that said BEWARE.

This time he had actually gone to sleep and was gently snoring when "HIIIIIII TOMMMMMM!" rang out once more.

"That does it!" howled the hermit. He ran out of the cave, dancing up and down in rage and shaking his fist at the sunny blue sky as if he thought that were to blame. He stomped his feet, gritted his teeth, and made such a terrible scene that a wind blew up, the leaves on the trees trembled, and thick black thunderclouds rolled in over Hermit Mountain.

"Now I feel a mite better," the old man said with a sniff. "But I won't feel real chipper till I find out who in tarnation's to blame for this confounded noise and put a stop to it!"

So, with a terrible frown, he picked up a thick knobby walking stick and a large empty flour sack he felt might come in handy and set out through the underbrush.

22

It did not take him long to find the place where the resounding echoes were coming from. As he came closer and closer to Tom's echo place, the old hermit quit stomping his feet and began to tread softly and lightly so that he made no noise and left no tracks.

Parting the branches of a large blueberry bush, he peered out and spied Tom and Trailer just sitting back enjoying those echoes!

The old man was about to spring out from the underbrush with a terrible roar and chase them from the spot when the black clouds closed out the blue sky and the first rain began to fall.

24

Before the hermit could make a move, the roll of thunder and lightning crashed above, sending Tom and Trailer dashing for home to escape the rain.

"You'd better not come back here!" the old hermit shouted after them, but his voice was lost in a big peal of thunder. Then he hurriedly crawled under a thick blueberry bush to get out of the rain himself. He felt better, but as he sat there he realized that Tom and Trailer would come back as long as there were echoes about. While he was thinking over the situation, his eyes fell on the large empty flour sack he had brought with him and suddenly he knew just how he would get rid of Tom, Trailer, and all the echoes!

25

When the storm blew over, the old man took up his stick and flour sack and carefully made his way in the dusky twilight to every nook and cranny, every deep ravine and crevice, between Hermit Mountain, Blueberry Mountain, Blackberry Mountain, Huckleberry Mountain, Raspberry Mountain, Strawberry Mountain, and Elderberry Mountain.

26

It took him a long, long time. He had to coax echoes out of the nooks of Blueberry Mountain. He had to pry echoes out of the crannies of Blackberry Mountain. He had to pull echoes out of the deep ravines of Huckleberry Mountain. He had to poke echoes out of the crevices of Raspberry Mountain. He had to drag echoes out of the caves of Strawberry Mountain. He even had to push echoes out of the gullies of Elderberry Mountain.

When the hermit had finished, it was pitch-black night but he had gathered up every echo, large and small, and stuffed it into the large flour sack which he tied with heavy string. It ballooned out over his shoulder as he carried it home. Back in his cave, he weighted the sack down with rocks while he ate his supper and then climbed into bed.

All was quiet in the dark cave, but before long the hermit sat up, scratched his head, and thought for a moment. Then he chuckled.

"Why not?" he asked himself hopping out of bed. He took the heavy rocks off the flour sack and popped back into his bed of pine boughs — using the billowing sack of echoes for a pillow!

28

The next day Tom and Trailer hurried to the echo place as soon as school was out. Tom took a deep breath, rar'ed back, and called out "HIIIIII TOMMMMM" as long and as loud as he could. Nothing happened.

30

Tom raised his eyebrows and looked at Trailer. Trailer raised his floppy ears and looked at Tom. The boy tried again but still nothing happened.

"Gosh all hemlock!" cried Tom. "There isn't a single echo left. What could have happened to them?"

Trailer was paying him no mind. Sniffing around the blueberry bushes, he soon found the trail of the hermit.

With a bay of discovery, the hound led Tom the way the old man had gone. They climbed up and down looking in every nook on Blueberry Mountain. They tramped up and down looking in every cranny on Blackberry Mountain. They hiked up and down looking in every deep ravine on Huckleberry Mountain. They trudged up and down looking in every crevice on Raspberry Mountain. They crawled up and down looking in every cave on Strawberry Mountain. They even puffed their way up and down looking in every gully on Elderberry Mountain. And, although they found plenty of blueberries, blackberries, huckleberries, raspberries, strawberries, and elderberries, not one echo could they discover.

The search took them a long, long time, It took so long, in fact, that Tom was beginning to think Trailer had lost his senses. Just then Trailer led him through some bushes and there was the hermit's cave. When Tom looked inside he could hardly believe his eyes.

There was the old man fast asleep in the middle of his afternoon nap with his head on a billowing flour sack.

Tom crept back to where Trailer was waiting proudly.

"Good work, old boy," Tom whispered, giving him a hug. "That flour sack must be full of echoes. With your help maybe we can get them back where they belong."

Silently they entered the cave, but just as Tom was reaching for the flour sack he stumbled over the hermit's knobby walking stick. It rolled away with a loud clatter!

"What's that?" shouted the hermit, leaping out of bed.

As he did so, the sack of echoes flew up behind him and began bouncing, bounding, and billowing all over the cave.

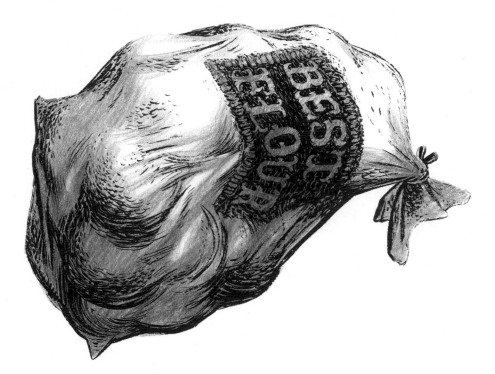

"Catch it, Trailer!" cried Tom. The dog leaped forward and caught hold of the edge of the flour sack with his teeth. When he did this the cloth tore apart with a sudden rip. And when the flour sack ripped, there exploded within that cave the largest, longest, most thunderous "HIIIIIIIII TOMMMMMMMM" that anyone has ever heard, before or since!

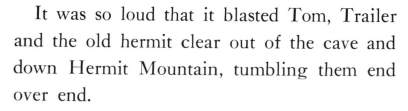

It was so loud that it blasted Tom, Trailer and the old hermit clear out of the cave and down Hermit Mountain, tumbling them end over end.

Once out in the open it separated into all the echoes, large and small, of Blueberry, Blackberry, Huckleberry, Raspberry, Strawberry, and Elderberry mountains, and each one bounded away to its own nook and canny once again.

38

Halfway down Hermit Mountain, Tom and the old man sat up rubbing their heads while Trailer shook himself once or twice. They weren't much hurt, just bruised and shaken. In fact, it wasn't three seconds before the hermit leaped up, hopping mad.

"What do you mean by this, you young whippersnapper?" he cried, shaking his fist at Tom. "Dag nab it, can't an old man ever get any peace and quiet? Why do you think I left town and climbed up this consarned mountain to live in a cave? Only so I could have things QUIET!" he finished with a roar.

Tom raised his eyebrows and looked at the hermit. Trailer raised his floppy ears and looked at the hermit.

40

Then the boy said slowly, "I like to listen to the echoes 'cause it makes me feel less lonesome. Makes me feel that my friends are standing on the mountain tops shouting: 'Hi Tom.' I didn't think there was anybody sleeping on the mountain in the afternoon. I'm surely sorry about it all, sir."

The old man calmed down a little at these mannerly words. "Harumph," he said, "perhaps I was a little hasty but I do have to have my nap."

Tom wrinkled up his brow. "Beg your pardon, sir," he said, "but why do you have to sleep all afternoon?"

"Don't ask silly questions," snapped the hermit. "I sleep all afternoon because — well, because — ". He stopped suddenly, looking rather astonished. "Why, I suppose because I have nothing else to do," he finished slowly.

Tom pulled his left ear. "Why is that, sir?" he asked thoughtfully.

"Dag nab it," fumed the hermit. "In the morning I hoe my turnips, pick berries, and hunt squirrels. In the afternoon there's nothing left to do."

Tom leaped up with a grin. "Gosh all hemlock, I have an idea!"

"What's that?" asked the old man suspiciously.

42

"Well, if you were to take a short nap in the afternoon and then walk down the mountain, you could meet me coming home from school."

"What would I want to do that for?" growled the old man.

"So you could ask me what I did at school and show me how to hunt squirrels and walk softly without leaving any tracks and — even maybe show me how you make the wind blow, the rain fall, or the snow fly!" Tom's grin was wider than ever. "And sometimes we could go up to my Echo Place, rar' back, call out our names, and make plenty of echoes!"

He turned to the old man suddenly. "You do have a name, don't you?"

"Now look here, you young whippersnapper — " Then the hermit broke off and sort of
grinned. "Sure, I have a name, son. It's John.
And you might have a pretty good idea there,
you just might!"

They shook hands and Trailer wagged his
tail happily.

44

So, every day now, when Tom says good bye
to his friends, he isn't lonesome at all as he
crosses the valley. On the other side, John, the
hermit, is waiting at the foot of the mountain.
He waves and grins and asks Tom how his
day has gone. Then they start up the mountain
with Trailer. The old man shows Tom how to
hunt squirrels and walk softly without leaving
any tracks and — even sometimes how he
makes the wind blow, the rain fall, or the snow
fly!

46

Every once in a while they go up to Tom's echo place. The old hermit looks out at all the mountaintops, rar's back and gives a long call. Then Tom rar's back and gives a long call.

Suddenly from every nook and cranny the echoes bounce around them: "Hi John, HII JOHN, HIIIIIII JOHNNNNNNN!"

"HI TOMM, HIII TOMMMM, HIIIII TOMMMMMMMM!"

And the old man, the boy, and the dog just
sit back and listen and listen and listen.

48